A Note to Parents

Welcome to REAL KIDS READERS, a series of phonics-based books for children who are beginning to read. In the classroom, educators use phonics to teach children how to sound out unfamiliar words, providing a firm foundation for reading skills. At home, you can use REAL KIDS READERS to reinforce and build on that foundation, because the books follow the same basic phonic guidelines that children learn in school.

Of course the best way to help your child become a good reader is to make the experience fun—and REAL KIDS READERS do that, too. With their realistic story lines and lively characters, the books engage children's imaginations. With their clean design and sparkling photographs, they provide picture clues that help new readers decipher the text. The combination is sure to entertain young children and make them truly want to read.

REAL KIDS READERS have been developed at three distinct levels to make it easy for children to read at their own pace.

- LEVEL 1 is for children who are just beginning to read.
- LEVEL 2 is for children who can read with help.
- LEVEL 3 is for children who can read on their own.

A controlled vocabulary provides the framework at each level. Repetition, rhyme, and humor help increase word skills. Because children can understand the words and follow the stories, they quickly develop confidence. They go back to each book again and again, increasing their proficiency and sense of accomplishment, until they're ready to move on to the next level. The result is a rich and rewarding experience that will help them develop a lifelong love of reading.

For my loving Omi
—L. P.

Special thanks to Lands' End, Dodgeville, WI, for providing
clothing; to East End Sporting Goods, Mattituck, NY, and to
Supreme Skateboard, NYC, for providing sports equipment;
and to James Adams and Julianna Carlson.

Produced by DWAI / Seventeenth Street Productions, Inc.
Reading Specialist: Virginia Grant Clammer

Library of Congress Cataloging-in-Publication Data
Papademetriou, Lisa.
  My pen pal, Pat / Lisa Papademetriou ; photographs by Dorothy Handelman.
      p.   cm.
  Summary: Pat has a pen pal who shares her name and many of the same interests,
but when the two Pats meet they are both in for a big surprise.
  ISBN 0-7613-2023-7 (lib. bdg.). — ISBN 0-7613-2048-2 (pbk.)
  [1. Pen pals—Fiction. 2. Sex role—Fiction. 3. Letters—Fiction] I. Handelman, Dorothy, ill.
II. Title.
PZ7.P1954My   1998
[E]—dc21
                                                          98-16596
                                                          CIP
                                                          AC

pbk: 10 9 8 7 6 5 4 3 2 1
lib: 10 9 8 7 6 5 4 3 2 1

My Pen Pal, Pat

By Lisa Papademetriou
Photographs by Dorothy Handelman

M

The Millbrook Press
Brookfield, Connecticut

"Listen up, class!" Mr. Davis said on Monday. "I have a surprise for you."

Patricia Scott sat up very straight at her desk. Her teacher's surprises were always good.

"Who knows what a pen pal is?" asked Mr. Davis.

Pat raised her hand high.

"Yes, Pat?" said Mr. Davis.

"A pen pal is someone you write letters to, but you've never met," said Pat.

"That's right," said Mr. Davis, "and that's my surprise. Each of you gets to be pen pals with someone from Ms. Corbett's class in Boston!"

Pat and the other kids cheered.

Mr. Davis held up some cards like a fan. "Each of these cards has a pen pal's name and address on it," he said. "You can come up one by one to pick a card. Then you can start writing your letter to your new pen pal."

"I wonder what the person I choose will be like," thought Pat. "I hope she's nice, and I hope she likes the same things I do!"

Finally it was her turn to pick a card. She took one look at the name on the back and blinked in surprise.

"Hey!" she said. "I picked Pat Glenn. My pen pal and I have the same first name!"

"That's great," said Mr. Davis. "You have something in common already.

Pat spent a lot of time on her letter. She tried hard, but her writing was kind of messy. At least she spelled everything correctly.

"Being a pen pal is cool," she thought. She hoped her new pen pal, Pat, would think so too.

When everyone was finished writing, Mr. Davis collected the letters. At the end of the school day, he put them in the mailbox.

On Wednesday, Patrick Glenn hurried home from school. His teacher, Ms. Corbett, had told the class that their pen pal letters would arrive soon. He couldn't wait to check the mail.

Sure enough, there it was—a letter with his name on it! Pat looked at the envelope. The writing on the front was kind of messy. But there was a really cool picture drawn on the back.

13

Pat tore open the envelope and read the letter.

Dear Pat,
  Hi! How are you? Guess what?
My name is Pat too! I am
8 years old, and I have light
brown hair and greenish eyes.
I live in New York City.
  Do you like to play baseball?
I play shortstop for my team.
I have a dog. His name is
Toby. Please write back!

                    Your Friend,
                    Pat

Toby ↑

15

"I can't believe it. My pen pal's name is Pat too!" thought Pat.

He tried to picture what Pat looked like. Was he tall or short, fat or thin?

"Maybe he looks a little like me," thought Pat.

Pat imagined playing baseball with his pen pal. If only they could meet in person. Pat was sure that they would be best friends.

Pat went upstairs to his room. He sat down at his desk and started writing to his pen pal. He wanted to finish the letter before dinner, so he had to start right away! He wondered how long it would take to get another letter from Pat.

Three days later, Pat got her first letter from her pen pal.

Dear Pat,

Hi pen pal. We are really alike! I love baseball, and I have the same color hair and eyes as you. But there's one way we're different. My mom is allergic to dogs, so I only have a turtle—and he bites.

I have to go now. Mom is making pizza tonight, and she lets me roll out the crust. When she isn't looking, I sneak bites of cheese. Yum!

Write back soon.

Your friend,
Pat

Pat smiled. Her pen pal's letter was funny. It was also very neat.

"Maybe she could teach me to write the way she does," Pat thought. "Then Mr. Davis wouldn't bug me about my messy writing."

She tried to imagine what her pen pal looked like. "I bet she looks something like me," she decided. She pictured the two of them making pizza. That would be fun! Too bad they didn't live in the same city.

Pat cleared a spot at the kitchen table. She got out a pencil and some paper. Then she sat down to write another letter to her pen pal.

But what should she say? She tapped her pencil on the table. She scratched an itch on her knee. Ouch! She'd scraped that spot the day before, and it still hurt. But at least now she knew what to write about.

As Pat finished her letter, her stomach started to rumble. "Hey, Dad!" she called. "Can we have pizza for dinner?"

Pat opened the second letter from his pen pal. It was a little bit longer than the first one—but not any neater.

Dear Pat,
Thanks for your letter. It made me hungry.
Yesterday we went to the park. I fell off my skateboard and got a huge scrape on my knee. You should see it. It's bigger than a baseball.
I yelled when my dad cleaned it, and my older sister called me a baby. She is such a pain! Do you have any brothers or sisters?

Your friend,
Pat

Tyrano-sister →

Pat folded up the letter. "Too bad Pat fell off his skateboard," he thought. "He must have been trying out a new trick."

Pat wished they lived in the same city. Then his pen pal could teach him how to skateboard.

He pictured the two of them riding side by side. That would be great! But if they lived in the same city, they wouldn't be pen pals.

Pat poured himself a glass of milk. He got out some bread and jam and made a sandwich. Then he sat down and wrote back to his pen pal.

A little jam got on the paper by accident. He hoped Pat wouldn't mind.

Dear Pat,
   Yes, I do have a little brother. He's the worst! Last night, I was trying to watch a scary movie on T.V. But he kept jumping out at me and yelling BOO! It was a great movie until he messed it up. Plus, he took my yo-yo and cut off the string. He said it looked better that way. Can you believe it! He is so weird.

Your friend,
Pat

A few days later, Pat got a letter from her pen pal. "That's funny," she said. "It smells yummy—like jam."

She opened the envelope and read the letter. "Poor Pat," she thought. "Her brother is as bad as my sister."

She imagined building a fort with her pen pal. They wouldn't allow any brothers or sisters inside. And if they had enough books and snacks, they would never have to leave.

Just then, Pat's dad came into the room. "Hi, Pat," he said. "Is that another letter from your pen pal?"

"Yes," said Pat. "I wish I could meet her. She sounds so neat."

"Well, maybe I can make your wish come true," said her dad. "I have to go to Boston for business next weekend. Would you like to come along and visit your friend?"

Pat's eyes opened wide. "Oh, Dad! I'd love to!" she cried. "And I know the perfect present to take along."

Pat couldn't believe the great letter his pen pal had sent him. He read it again to make sure he wasn't dreaming.

Dear Pat,

Guess what? I'm coming for a visit. My dad has a business trip to Boston next weekend, and I get to come along. That means that we can meet in person. If it's okay, I'll come to your house, at 3:00 P.M. on Saturday. See you then. I can't wait!

Your friend,
Pat

P.S. I'm sorry about your yo-yo. My sister has a really cool one, but she won't let me use it.

My backpack is already packed for Boston!

Pat felt like cheering. His pen pal, Pat, was coming for a visit! They would have so much fun together. After all, they were almost best friends already.

"I better check with Mom!" thought Pat, and he rushed off to find her.

The rest of the week went by very slowly. By Saturday, Pat felt as if he'd been waiting *forever.*

He picked up the present he had bought for Pat and put it down again. "Pat's late," he said to his mother.

"He's only two minutes late," his mom pointed out. "I'm sure he'll be here soon."

Just then, the doorbell rang.

Pat picked up his present and ran for the door. "I'll get it!" he yelled.

His mom grinned. "I'm sure you will," she said, following behind him.

Pat flung the door open wide.

Pat and Pat stared at each other. For a moment, nobody spoke.

"Pat?" said Patrick.

"Pat?" said Patricia.

"That's Pat?" said Pat's mom.

"That's Pat?" said Pat's dad.

"I was kind of expecting someone . . . different," Patrick said.

Patricia nodded. "Me too," she said.

Patrick didn't know what to say next. "I can't believe my pen pal is a girl," he thought. "We aren't alike at all."

Patricia looked at her feet. "I can't believe Pat is a boy," she thought. "We don't have anything in common."

Then she remembered the present she had brought. "Here. This is for you," she said. She held out a small package.

"I have something for you too," said Patrick. He held out his gift.

They traded packages. Patricia shook hers. "What is it?" she asked.

"It's a yo-yo," Patrick said.

Patricia started to laugh.

"What's so funny?" Patrick asked.

Patricia pointed to the package in his hand. "That's a yo-yo too," she said.

Patrick and Patricia both grinned. Maybe they were alike after all.

"Let's try them out," said Patrick.

"Okay," said Patricia. "Then we can play catch."

"Sure," said Patrick. "And then we can make pizza."

So that's just what Pat and Pat did.

Reading with Your Child

Even though your child is reading more independently now, it is vital that you continue to take part in this important learning experience.

- Try to read with your child at least twenty minutes each day, as part of your regular routine.
- Encourage your child to keep favorite books in one convenient, cozy spot, so you don't waste valuable reading time looking for them.
- Read and familiarize yourself with the Phonic Guidelines on the next pages.
- Praise your young reader. Be the cheerleader, not the teacher. Your enthusiasm and encouragement are key ingredients in your child's success.

What to Do if Your Child Gets Stuck on a Word

- Wait a moment to see if he or she works it out alone.
- Help him or her decode the word phonetically. Say, "Try to sound it out."
- Encourage him or her to use picture clues. Say, "What does the picture show?"
- Encourage him or her to use context clues. Say, "What would make sense?"
- Ask him or her to try again. Say, "Read the sentence again and start the tricky word. Get your mouth ready to say it."
- If your child still doesn't "get" the word, tell him or her what it is. Don't wait for frustration to build.

What to Do if Your Child Makes a Mistake

- If the mistake makes sense, ignore it—unless it is part of a pattern of errors you wish to correct.
- If the mistake doesn't make sense, wait a moment to see if your child corrects it.
- If your child doesn't correct the mistake, ask him or her to try again, either by decoding the word or by using context or picture clues. Say, "Get your mouth ready" or "Make it sound right" or "Make it make sense."
- If your child still doesn't "get" the word, tell him or her what it is. Don't wait for frustration to build.